UNICORN HANDBOOK

BY BRANDON T. SNIDER

CARTOON
NETWORK
BOOKS

AN IMPRINT OF PENGUIN RANDOM HOUSE

CARTOON NETWORK BOOKS
Penguin Young Readers Group
An Imprint of Penguin Random House LLC

Additional illustrations by Paulina Ganucheau.

ISBN 9780515157567   10 9 8 7 6 5 4 3 2 1

Table of Contents

Friendship & Fun   8

Appearance   10

Compliments   13

Daily Affirmations   14

A Friend in Need   17

Friendship Quiz   18

Badge Checklist   23

Release Your Fierceness   28

Skills   30

Stand Up for Yourself!   32

Sanctuary   35

Fierceness Quiz   36

Badge Checklist   41

Leadership   46

Goals   48

Advice   50

Leadership Quiz   54

Badge Checklist   59

Favorites   62

More Daily Affirmations   64

What Do You Do?   66

Art Break!   68

A Letter to . . .   72

Scrapbook   74

Final Badge Checklist   76

Anyway! I'm here to show you all the ins and outs of #UnicornLife. I know a lot of stuff about unicorns, probably more than anyone I know. And I'm here to teach you all about it.

Let's begin, shall we?

The first lesson is—you mess with the unicorn, YOU GET THE HORN!

Your second lesson is . . .

NOT SO FAST, DONNY!

Who said that?!

Hey, Donny! How's our favorite unicorn?

It's going great, but you know it takes a lot of work to keep my horn this shiny.

Like polishing it?

Yes, but having a SUPER SWEET horn is only a part of being a unicorn. We also have lots of OFFICIAL training and we have to earn badges!

I want to earn unicorn badges, too! Can you train me?

Of course! But I'm going to need some help from your sisters.

Blossom and Buttercup, will you help me train? Pleeeeeeease . . .

As long as it's hard and requires you to be tough, you bet!

Let's do it!

Are you ready to start your training?

Friendship & Fun

It's time for FRIENDSHIP & FUN! That's a big part of being a unicorn. But first you're going to need a strong MOTTO!

Is that a fancy hat or a type of exotic fish???

What? No. A motto is a short sentence or phrase that outlines what you're all about.

Oh cool! You mean like, "I'm Bubbles, and I'm a Powerpuff Girl!"

A little less obvious, but you're on the right track.

"I hope you like to laugh, because BUBBLES is handing out giggles ALL DAY LONG!"

That one's got major POWFACTOR!

Okay, so, mine might need some work, but that's why we're here! Try coming up with a bunch of different mottos that fit your unique personality.

Mottos

....

....

....

....

....

....

....

....

....

....

....

....

....

Appearance

Unicorns should always feel confident. They should express themselves!

How do you express yourself, Donny?

I think it's totally fun to experiment with different looks! Let's try some out by coloring in these selfies!

Oooo. I really like this one!

Make a list of things you like about your appearance. Do you love how frizzy your hair gets when it rains? Do you have a fancy mole on your arm? WRITE IT DOWN!

I love my unicorn horn!

Yeah, so do we!

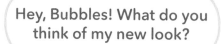

Compliments

A unicorn should always know how to take a compliment. How should you respond to these?

This mane of yours is so luxurious, like the wind.

....

....

Donny, you're just as sweet as cherry pie!

....

....

You've got SUCH a nice smile.
It really lights up your mouth.

....

....

Nice horn!

....

....

Daily Affirmations

LISTEN UP! We all have bad days . . .

Tell me about it!

But it's important for a unicorn to recognize those feelings and make the best of it with DAILY AFFIRMATIONS!

I don't know what those are.

A daily affirmation is a little truth that we say out loud in order to motivate us to be our best! Here, I'll show you. "Bubbles, you are hilarious! Your jokes make EVERYONE laugh, and laughter is the best medicine!

Also, your pigtails are cute."

Can I try? "Hey, Donny! YOU'RE A UNICORN AND I LOVE YOU!"

Ummm, that's a start. Let's come up with more!

....

....

....

....

....

....

....

....

....

....

....

....

Are you having fun yet, Bubbles?

Of course! But being a unicorn takes lots of work!

That's true. Fortunately, I've got lots of great friends to lean on, and so do you. You never know what kinds of things other people are going through just by looking at them. EVERYONE has struggles, after all.

Yup. Even Powerpuff Girls!

Unicorns, too! That's why this activity is really important, so listen up.

A Friend in Need

Write about a time that you helped
a friend in need. Did you help someone when
they were struggling? Did you help out a pal
when they were being picked on? Talk about those
experiences. And if you've never helped a friend in
need, then what are you waiting for?
GO DO IT! (It'll feel really good.)

Friendship Quiz

Friendship Quiz Time!

Let's do it!

Q: Which member of the SENSITIVE THUGZ are you?

A. Chance

B. Dax

C. OMG THERE ARE OTHER MEMBERS?!
   I ONLY HAVE EYES FOR CHANCE AND DAX!

D: My parents won't let me listen to music.

Q: When something good happens to a friend of yours how does it make you feel? Why do you think it makes you feel that way?

....

....

....

Q: OH NO! Your best friend had a terrible day. How would you cheer them up?

....

....

Q: List three nice things you can do to show a friend how much you care for them.

....

....

....

Q: Why is it good to help people when they ask for it?

....

....

....

Q: What are four characteristics of a true friend?

....

....

....

....

Fill this box with all kinds of tiny little unicorns!

Is this really part of the test? I love drawing unicorns!

YES! AND IT'S VERY IMPORTANT! NOW DRAW THOSE TINY LITTLE UNICORNS.

Q: If you had a beauty blog, which of these things would you make a video about?

A. The wrong way to brush your pigtails

B. Powder blue: THE BEST COLOR EVER!

C. Cleaning your skirt after a fierce battle

D. Trying out a new look for summer

Q: Uh-oh. You and your friend had a disagreement, and now you're both angry at each other. What steps will you take to settle your differences?

....

....

....

Q: If Bubbles was going to have an AWESOME new catchphrase, what would it be?

....

....

Q: Should Bubbles switch her pigtails out for one strong braid? Why or why not? COMPLETE ANSWERS, PLEASE.

....

....

....

This quiz was so much fun, Donny! Was it all part of being a unicorn?

I'm glad you liked it. I also threw some other questions and stuff in there that I was just curious about. You know, research and stuff.

Isn't there supposed to be an answer key so I can see if I got the right answers?

Nope, sometimes unicorns just like to ask questions and see what happens!

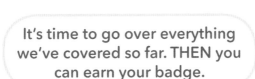

It's time to go over everything we've covered so far. THEN you can earn your badge.

I GET A BADGE!? THAT'S AWESOME!!!!

It's totally awesome! (To earn your unicorn badge you have to complete all the activities first.)

This is the best day ever!

Badge Checklist

___ Created a unicorn motto

___ Helped a unicorn try out a new look

___ Made a list of stuff you like about your appearance

___ Learned how to take a compliment

___ Wrote some daily affirmations

___ Talked about a time that you helped someone

___ Completed the Friendship Quiz

___ Promised Donny you would take him to a water park

(That last one is just a suggestion.)
Did you complete all the stuff above?
Then BADGE UNLOCKED!

We had some GOOD TIMES, didn't we, Bubbles?

I learned so much! I can't believe my unicorn training is already finished.

Well, not quite . . . Write about an AMAZING time when YOU learned something new.

....

....

....

....

....

....

....

....

....

....

I love unicorns. I wonder what Donny is thinking about.

Draw what Donny is thinking above and describe it below.

PARTY TIME IS OVER!

Whoa! Hey, Buttercup. Are you here to congratulate me on becoming a unicorn? I just did all the fun tests and stuff with Donny. I got a badge! Hey, I'm getting kind of hungry. When's snack time?

There's no time for snacks! Now we begin the NEXT PHASE of your training.

Next phase?! How many more phases are there? I was really hoping I could take a break and play with my unicorn friends.

Being a unicorn isn't all fun, games, and cherry pie. Cut the DRAMABOMB and let's GET TO WORK!

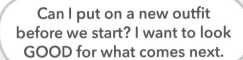

Can I put on a new outfit before we start? I want to look GOOD for what comes next.

Sigh. Sure. Color in a brand-new look for Bubbles here.

Release Your Fierceness

Every unicorn needs to be FIERCE!

YIKES! I don't want to be mean to people. I want to be a unicorn, not a scary tiger or something.

Being fierce isn't about being mean or scary, Bubbles. FIERCENESS is being passionate and enthusiastic about something you love. What is something you're FIERCELY passionate about?

Unicorns!

Sure, I guess that works. But let's come up with something else just to be safe. Being FIERCE is being BOLD and standing out from the crowd.

What do you do to be FIERCE? Do you stand up to bullies when they pick on people? Do you try new foods even though they look weird?

I hugged someone too hard once!

List some FIERCE things that you've done.

- -

- -

- -

- -

- -

- -

- -

- -

- -

- -

Skills

Hold on to your hat, Bubbles. We're going to start moving FAST!

I'm not wearing a hat! Should I be wearing a hat? (Someone draw me a hat!)

EVERYONE is good at something. Can you give a kitty cat a bath without getting scratched? Can you make a delicious stack of pancakes? List some stuff that you're good at doing!

_____

_____

_____

_____

_____

_____

_____

What are some things you WANT to be good at but are still learning about? List them!

I want to learn how to ride a bike! And knit a scarf! And braid a—

WRITE THESE DOWN, BUBBLES.

Stand Up for Yourself!

There might be people out there
who won't understand you until they get to
see how cool you are up close and personal.
A unicorn has got to be TOUGH.
Write about a time when you stood
up for yourself.

It's time for a problem-solving activity. BUCKLE UP!

Why? Are we going somewhere? Should I wear my new outfit and hat? I'M NOT PREPARED.

Calm down, Bubbles. We aren't going anywhere. Take a look at the situation below and talk about how you would handle it. Would you unleash your FIERCENESS? Once you've written your answer, talk it over with an adult to see what they think.

Q: Frank, the new kid at school, is having trouble making friends. His new classmates constantly make fun of him for dressing differently and having a high voice. What would you do to make Frank feel better and more accepted? Would you use your FIERCENESS to stand up to his mean classmates?

All this training is making me sooo tired. I wish I had a special place to go where I could RELAX and be alone. I'd decorate it with all my favorite stuff! It would be my own little UNICORN SANCTUARY!

It's your lucky day, Bubbles. Feel free to turn this space into anything you want! Design it just the way you like it. And be quick, because we have some more work to do after this.

I'll paint stripes on the walls! And I'll get a new lamp! Maybe I'll put some posters up, too. OH, and a rug! I'll definitely need a rug. And some throw pillows.

Sanctuary

Where do YOU go to relax and be alone? Draw or describe it below.

Fierceness Quiz

Fierceness Quiz Time!

I'm going to ACE IT! I watched all the beauty blog videos and even practiced drawing tiny little unicorns when no one was looking.

Beauty blogs?! Tiny little unicorns?!?! HA! You won't find any of that stuff here!

Huh?!?! But I studied so good!

Q: LEARNING IS FIERCE. What are three fierce things you studied in school?

Q: LOVE IS FIERCE. Who are three fierce people you love?

We Powerpuff Girls have AURA POWERS that change shape based on our mood and personality. What does a unicorn aura look like, Bubbles? DRAW IT AND LET'S SEE!

I'll help!

Thanks, Donny!

Q: If you could have THREE DIFFERENT superpowers, what would they be?

Q: Who are three FIERCE people you look up to? What is so fierce about them?

Q: What's a good name for people who LOVE unicorns?

A. UNICORNIES

B. HORN LOVERS

C. THOSE PEOPLE

D. BRAHS

Q: Mojo Jojo wants to destroy Townsville! How will you use your fierceness to take him down? Will you try talking sense into him, or will you distract him with a funky dance? Describe your plan in as much detail as possible.

Do I know any funky dances?

Bubbles, EVERYONE knows at least one funky dance.

Time to go over our checklist and make sure you've completed all the tasks so you can earn your second badge.

ANOTHER BADGE?! I'M GOING TO BE PRINCESS OF THE UNICORNS! THIS IS SO EXCITING!

Not quite yet, Bubbles. There's still work to be done.

Badge Checklist

___ Created a brand-new look

___ Made a list of fierce qualities

___ Wrote about stuff that you're good at doing

___ Wrote about stuff that you'd like to be good at doing someday

___ Described a time when you stood up for yourself

___ Completed problem-solving activity

___ Drew a unicorn sanctuary

___ Completed the Fierceness Quiz

If you've completed all the stuff above, then consider your BADGE UNLOCKED! (And if you haven't completed all that stuff, then what are you waiting for?!?! Becoming a unicorn is serious business!)

Oh no! There's one last mission I forgot about! All these villains are attacking Townsville, and the only thing that can stop them are SASSY ZINGERS! Is there a heroic unicorn who can help defeat them?

Don't worry, Buttercup. Those aren't really bad guys. They're just cardboard cutouts.

I know that, Bubbles. Just pretend they're real for now and come up with some SASSY ZINGERS!

You've trained with the rest, now train with THE BEST!

Oh wow! Does that mean the PRINCEQUEEN OF UNICORNIA is going to train me? OH BOY, OH BOY, OH BOY!

First of all, is that a real unicorn title?! Second of all, I WAS REFERRING TO ME!

Oh, Blossom. Can I take a nap now? I really need my beauty rest.

WAKE UP, SLEEPYHEAD! You've got to stay ALERT.

What kinds of things can you do to keep your mind SHARP?

Read books!

Very good answer.

Try new things!

Another solid answer. You've GOT to keep your brain growing nice and strong. There are always new things to LEARN! Write about some of the things you think you might want to learn more about.

~~~~~~~~~~~~~~~~~~~~~~~~~~~~

~~~~~~~~~~~~~~~~~~~~~~~~~~~~

~~~~~~~~~~~~~~~~~~~~~~~~~~~~

~~~~~~~~~~~~~~~~~~~~~~~~~~~~

~~~~~~~~~~~~~~~~~~~~~~~~~~~~

~~~~~~~~~~~~~~~~~~~~~~~~~~~~

~~~~~~~~~~~~~~~~~~~~~~~~~~~~

~~~~~~~~~~~~~~~~~~~~~~~~~~~~

LEADERSHIP

Listen very carefully, Bubbles. I'll only say this once—EVERYONE can be a LEADER! Leading isn't just about being in charge of others, it's about setting a GOOD EXAMPLE for people to follow.

So being a leader isn't about telling people what to do?

Of course not! A leader should be FAIR, HONEST, CONFIDENT, COMMITTED, POSITIVE, CREATIVE, INSPIRING, and APPROACHABLE.

That's A LOT to think about.

It sure is. So think REALLY HARD about what it means to be each of these things, and describe your thoughts in the space provided.

FAIR

HONEST

CONFIDENT

COMMITTED

POSITIVE

CREATIVE

INSPIRING

APPROACHABLE

GOALS

What are your goals, Bubbles?

To become the best unicorn I can be!

Okay . . . anything else?

Uh . . . well . . . I guess . . .

Time to get SERIOUS!

AAAHHH!

I didn't mean to startle you, but setting goals is an important thing to do. It gives you something positive to work toward and achieve. A short-term goal is something you'd like to do in the near future, like ride a bike or put ketchup on your scrambled eggs (which is gross, by the way). A long-term goal is something you'd like to do years into the future, like own a luxury boat or create world peace.

Oooo! World peace would be great, I think!

Me too. Now think of some goals, and write about the steps you would take to achieve them!

SHORT-TERM GOAL #1:
HOW WILL YOU ACHIEVE IT?

SHORT-TERM GOAL #2:
HOW WILL YOU ACHIEVE IT?

LONG-TERM GOAL:
HOW WILL YOU ACHIEVE IT?

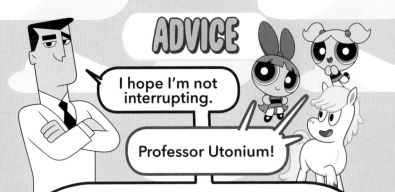

ADVICE

I hope I'm not interrupting.

Professor Utonium!

I overheard Blossom talking about leadership earlier. You know, ever since the Powerpuff Girls came into my life, I've come to realize how important it is to set a good example for them. These girls can be a bit of a handful at times, but I'm always happy to share some good advice to help them along their way.

ADVICE is a valuable suggestion you give someone to guide them in a positive direction. Think of it as a helpful hint!

THAT gives me an idea! Write about some GOOD ADVICE you've received from a friend or a relative. What was it?

Write about some BAD ADVICE you've received from a friend or a relative. What was it? Did you take the bad advice? What happened next?

~~~~~~

~~~~~~

~~~~~~

~~~~~~

~~~~~~

~~~~~~

~~~~~~

~~~~~~

~~~~~~

~~~~~~

SO MANY QUESTIONS!

Sorry, Bubbles, but inquiring minds want to know.

I'm sure you've learned a thing or two during your journey. It's time to write about it! What's some good advice that YOU might give someone who asks?

~~~~~~

~~~~~~

~~~~~~

I've got some good advice. Don't eat the yellow snow!

What's some silly advice you might give someone? GO WILD and come up with whatever funny stuff you can think of!

~~~~~~

~~~~~~

~~~~~~

Rely on your friends!

Always have a bucket of Unicorn Polish nearby! You never know when your coat will need it!

Bubbles and Donny are so tired from training that they're taking a quick unicorn nap. I can't wait to wake them up! I bet they're having some wild and wonderful dreams. If only we could see them . . .

LEADERSHIP QUIZ

WAKE UP!
It's Leadership Quiz time!

AAAHHH!!!
I'M AWAKE!

I don't know how the other girls ran their quizzes, but mine is going to be TOUGH, so get ready to be TESTED.

Q: A younger unicorn comes to you with a question. What do you do?

A. Tell them to go to an older unicorn because you're too busy right now.

B. Pretend like you're sleeping.

C. Answer their question to the best of your ability and try to help them as much as possible.

D. Run away.

Q: What is communication? Why is it important for unicorns to communicate with one another?

~~~~~~

~~~~~~

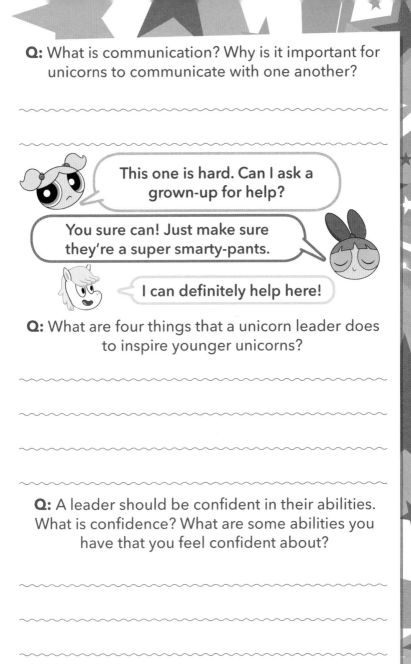

This one is hard. Can I ask a grown-up for help?

You sure can! Just make sure they're a super smarty-pants.

I can definitely help here!

Q: What are four things that a unicorn leader does to inspire younger unicorns?

~~~~~~

~~~~~~

~~~~~~

~~~~~~

Q: A leader should be confident in their abilities. What is confidence? What are some abilities you have that you feel confident about?

~~~~~~

~~~~~~

~~~~~~

Q: Which of these three people looks like the BEST leader?

Is this a trick question!?

NO!

Q: What does it mean to be COURAGEOUS?

A. It means you stand up for what's right, no matter the outcome!

B. It means you watch people stand up for what's right while you sit on the sidelines!

C. It means you stay at home and stare at the wall.

D. I don't know.

Leaders should always be organized.
How do you stay organized?

~~~~~~~~~~~~~~~~~~~~~~~~~~~~~~~~~~~~~

~~~~~~~~~~~~~~~~~~~~~~~~~~~~~~~~~~~~~

~~~~~~~~~~~~~~~~~~~~~~~~~~~~~~~~~~~~~

Q: Princess Morbucks is up to her old tricks! She thinks she can use her money to boss everyone around, but that's not how things work in Townsville. How would a STRONG LEADER handle this situation?

How I would deal with Princess Morbucks:

....

....

....

....

....

....

....

....

....

....

BADGE CHECKLIST

___ Wrote about stuff you'd like to learn more about

___ Described leadership terms

___ Created short-term goals

___ Created a long-term goal

___ Wrote about good advice you've received

___ Wrote about bad advice you've received

___ Listed some good advice and some silly advice

___ Completed the Leadership Quiz

Did you do all that stuff? If so, then BADGE UNLOCKED!

As a special treat, you and Donny get to create your very own DONNYMOBILE!

YEAH!!!

(Do unicorns need mobiles?)

You never know. It's ALWAYS good to be prepared. First, make a list of all the cool features it should have, and then draw it in the space provided.

The Donnymobile runs on SPARKLES! And you can only park it on a MOONBEAM!

~~~~~~~~~~~~~~~~~~~~~~~~~~~~~~~~~~~~~~

~~~~~~~~~~~~~~~~~~~~~~~~~~~~~~~~~~~~~~

~~~~~~~~~~~~~~~~~~~~~~~~~~~~~~~~~~~~~~

~~~~~~~~~~~~~~~~~~~~~~~~~~~~~~~~~~~~~~

~~~~~~~~~~~~~~~~~~~~~~~~~~~~~~~~~~~~~~

~~~~~~~~~~~~~~~~~~~~~~~~~~~~~~~~~~~~~~

Favorites

You're almost there, Bubbles!

Don't give up now!

YOU CAN DO IT!

I'm exhausted. I don't know if I can do any more training.

Stay focused. You're SO CLOSE. Think about how good it will feel to make it to the end. Maybe we'll even treat you to some of your favorite things.

LIKE ICE CREAM WITH SPRINKLES?!

You betcha!

List a bunch of your favorite things below

....

....

....

....

....

....

....

....

....

....

....

....

....

....

More Daily Affirmations

Remember how you wrote some daily affirmations before? Well, now that you've learned all kinds of new things, it's time to write some BRAND-NEW ONES. Keep them positive and inspiring.

....

....

....

....

....

....

....

....

....

....

....

My favorite daily affirmation is "Be nice to people even if they're being TOTAL BUTTZILLAS!"

My favorite is "BE FIERCE OR GO HOME, BUTTERCUP! ARE YOU LISTENING, BUTTERCUP? I'M TALKING TO YOU, BUTTERCUP!"

Whoa. That's kind of harsh.

I'm learning not to be so hard on myself.

Cool. I guess we ALL have something new to learn.

"Donny, you are a UNICORN and you are WORTH IT!"

WHAT DO YOU DO?

Oh no! An EVIL VILLAIN has taken over Townsville!

What do we do?

First, you've got to DESIGN this scary bad guy. Make 'em nice and creepy!

OKAY, OKAY, OKAY! THEN WHAT?!?

Calm down, Bubbles. Take a deep breath. This one is all about SAFETY. When bad stuff happens, sometimes people need assistance. How will you help the people of Townsville? Think of all the ways you can be of service, and list them below.

....

....

....

....

....

....

....

....

....

....

Art Break!

ART BREAK!!!

YEAH! ART! (Please, no more tough questions.)

If you're going to be a unicorn, you're going to need a personalized logo that captures your spirit and passion.

A SWEETEE STREAK!

Something like that. Use the space to come up with cool logo ideas!

THEN will I be a unicorn?!

Almost!

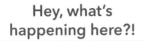

Hey, what's happening here?!

We had to give the Mayor of Townsville room to advertise his Pickle Museum. It's part of our contract.

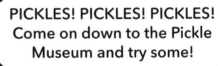

PICKLES! PICKLES! PICKLES! Come on down to the Pickle Museum and try some!

A Letter to . . .

It's time to get a little serious. Bubbles, when you first started your training, you were so young and inexperienced. You've come a long way!

I thought I knew EVERYTHING, but you all showed me that I had a lot of stuff to learn. And there's still more stuff out there that I don't even know!

There's always new stuff to learn about yourself AND the world around you.

Bubbles, it's time to write a letter to your younger self.

Yep! Think back to how you were thinking and feeling at the time and give yourself a little pep talk. Remind yourself that you've got a journey full of challenges ahead but you can achieve your GOALS! Think positively and remember that even though it might be hard sometimes, it's worth it in the end.

....

....

....

....

....

....

....

....

....

....

....

....

....

SCRAPBOOK

What are some of your favorite memories and moments? Use the space to make a scrapbook of images from the past.

You could even draw a moment or memory that you hope will happen in the future!

Like when I become the UNICORN SUPREME-O OF THE UNIVERSE!

Are you sure these are real unicorn titles?

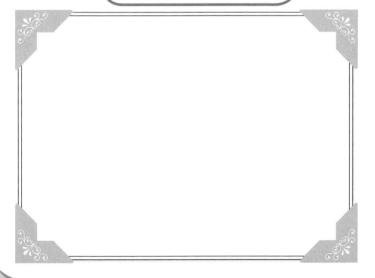

Remember that your past is part of your life but it doesn't define you!

YOU'RE SO CLOSE, BUBBLES! ALMOST THERE!

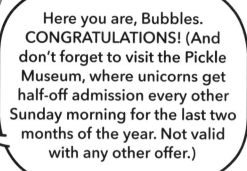

Here you are, Bubbles. CONGRATULATIONS! (And don't forget to visit the Pickle Museum, where unicorns get half-off admission every other Sunday morning for the last two months of the year. Not valid with any other offer.)

Final Badge Checklist

ALL BADGES EARNED!!!
UNICORN ACHIEVEMENT UNLOCKED!

WE'RE ALL SO
PROUD OF YOU!

THIS IS THE BEST
DAY OF MY LIFE!

I can't believe it. I'm finally, OFFICIALLY a unicorn. I trained my haunches off, but I just know there's more out there for me, and I can't wait to discover it. You taught me to love myself and others, to never give up, and whatever happens, DON'T BE A BUTTZILLA.

That's right, Bubbles. Life is a journey, so STRAP IN and get ready to ride.

I FEEL EMPOWERED!

Blossom, are you crying?

I just love happy endings!

This isn't an ENDING, it's a BEGINNING!

I can't believe we put this together so quickly. We should really run a unicorn-training school . . .